ISBN: 978-0-9844366-6-8

Library of Congress Control Number: 2009920258

First published in the United States in 2010
by Mathew Price Limited
12300 Ford Road, Dallas TX75234

Text and illustrations copyright © 2010 Atsuko Morozumi
Designed by Empire Design Studio
Manufactured in China

The ELVES' FIRST CHRISTMAS

THE UNTOLD STORY OF HOW THE ELVES FIRST MET SANTA

ATSUKO MOROZUMI

MP

MATHEW PRICE

Long ago a group of elves lived deep
in the forest. And they were happy.

Then one day, everything changed.
Men arrived with axes and saws and started cutting down
the trees. The elves watched as their homes were destroyed.

"Come," said Elwin, the chief elf. "We have to leave."

"Where are we going?" asked the elves.

"To find a place to live," said Elwin. "There must be a
place where men don't come."

And so their journey began.

After several weeks, they came to a forest, full of tall trees. But the forest floor was dark and no plants grew. "There is nothing to eat," one elf said. So they went on.

They found another forest close by. It was beautiful, but it was full of wild animals.

They hurried on.

They thought they had found the perfect place, just
like their own forest. But close by was a small village.
"Men will come," said Elwin. "We have to go on."

Avoiding towns and villages, the elves traveled north.
Autumn came and went.

One day snow began to fall.

Soon the snow was falling thick
and heavy and it grew dark.

The elves struggled on.

They saw a light in the distance and stopped.
"Come," said Elwin. "We have no choice,
we must find shelter."

The light was from a small farm.
Silently the elves crept into the barn.
They hid themselves in piles of hay
and quickly fell asleep.

Elwin tried to keep watch
but soon he, too, slept.

He woke up with a start. An old man with a lantern in his hand was bending over him. Elwin jumped up.

"Don't worry," said the old man gently, "you are quite safe here. What is your name?"

"El...Elwin," stammered the chief elf.

"I'm Santa Claus," said the old man, "and this is my wife."

"Why don't you come into the house?" said Mrs. Claus. "It's nice and warm in there."

Mrs. Claus gave the elves a hot meal and a comfortable place to rest.
Elwin explained to Santa about their search for a new home.
"Hmm," said Santa. "Let me think about that."

He showed Elwin his workshop.
"There's a lot of work here," said the chief elf.
"Perhaps," said Santa, "but it's good work. I love it."

The next day was cold and clear. Santa took
the elves and showed them his valley.

"This valley is protected," he said. "You would
be safe here."

"But we need trees," said Elwin, "big trees.
These are no good."

"Why not build houses?" said Santa. "I'll help you."

"I don't know," said Elwin. "We'll have to discuss it."

The elves lived with Santa and Mrs. Claus through the long hard winter and by the time spring came, it was agreed: they would stay. They began to build.

They worked hard. They were all anxious to get everything finished before the winter.

Hurry, hurry, hurry,
Before the land is white.
Build an elfin house
For a snowy night.

Santa taught them everything, from building snow-proof windows to fitting steam pipes.

As the first flakes of snow began to fall,
the Elfin Village was completed.

The elves held a big party.

In the midst of all the celebration, Elwin
noticed that Santa looked pale and worried.

"Are you feeling all right, Santa?" he asked.

"Tired," said Santa. "Just tired."

But that night, Santa fell ill.
His fever lasted for days.
The elves came to visit him
and then tiptoed away again.

"He's exhausted," said Mrs. Claus,
"and he's worried that there won't
be enough toys this Christmas."

"He spent too much time working
for us," said Elwin.

Slowly Santa recovered. One day he was
well enough to sit up in bed. But he was sad.
Christmas was coming and there were
not enough toys. Children would be
disappointed.

Then Elwin came to see him.

"Come with me," he said.
"I have something to show you."

He took Santa by the hand and led him into the Elfin
Great Hall. Toys lined every wall, row upon row.
The elves had turned it into a great toy workshop.

"But – this is wonderful," said Santa in amazement.

"You know how to build houses," said Elwin shyly.
"We know how to make toys."

When Christmas Eve came, Santa had plenty of toys to give, enough for every child. The elves helped him load the sleigh and watched as he set off on his journey across the world.

Every year the elves' Great Hall becomes a magical workshop where toys of every shape and size are made.

I think it always will.